FAMOUS PHARAOHS

Julia Wall

AF605709

Famous Pharaohs

Text: Julia Wall
Editor: Rebecca Crisp
Design: James Lowe
Series design: James Lowe
Photo researcher: Libby Henry
Production controllers: Renee Cusmano and Lisa Porter

Acknowledgements
The author and publisher would like to acknowledge permission to reproduce material from the following sources:
akg-images, London: p. 23; akg-images, London/Erich Lessing: p. 5 (bottom left); Corbis Australia: pp. 1, 5 (bottom middle), 15 (inset), 16–17, 8, 10, 11, 20 (left), 22 (left), cover; Erich Lessing: p. 9; Getty Images: pp. 3, 4 (top), 14 (inset), 19 (bottom), 20 (right), back cover; Guy Holt © Cengage Learning Australia: p. 4 (bottom); Photolibrary: pp. 5 (top and bottom right), 6, 7, 13, 14–15 (main), 18–19, 19 (top), 21 (top), 22 (right); © The Trustees of the British Museum, all rights reserved: p. 21 (bottom).

Every effort has been made to trace and acknowledge copyright. However, if any infringement has occurred the publishers tender their apologies and invite the copyright holders to contact them.

Fast Forward Independent Texts
Level 20

Text © 2009 Cengage Learning Australia Pty Limited
Illustrations © 2009 Cengage Learning Australia Pty Limited

Copyright Notice
This Work is copyright. No part of this Work may be reproduced, stored in a retrieval system, or transmitted in any form or by any means without prior written permission of the Publisher. Except as permitted under the *Copyright Act 1968*, for example any fair dealing for the purposes of private study, research, criticism or review, subject to certain limitations. These limitations include: Restricting the copying to a maximum of one chapter or 10% of this book, whichever is greater; Providing an appropriate notice and warning with the copies of the Work disseminated; Taking all reasonable steps to limit access to these copies to people authorised to receive these copies; Ensuring you hold the appropriate Licences issued by the Copyright Agency Limited ("CAL"), supply a remuneration notice to CAL and pay any required fees.

ISBN 978 0 17 018000 9
ISBN 978 0 17 017898 3 (set)

Cengage Learning Australia
Level 7, 80 Dorcas Street
South Melbourne, Victoria Australia 3205
Phone: 1300 790 853

Cengage Learning New Zealand
Unit 4B Rosedale Office Park
331 Rosedale Road, Albany, North Shore NZ 0632
Phone: 0800 449 725

For learning solutions, visit **cengage.com.au**

Printed in Australia by Ligare Pty Ltd
4 5 6 7 8 9 10 22 21 20 19 18

FAMOUS PHARAOHS

Julia Wall

Contents

The Great Pharaohs of Ancient Egypt

Ancient Egypt was ruled by kings, and some queens, called pharaohs. The pharaohs were very important to society and religion.

Pharaohs were mostly male, but when a woman ruled Egypt, she was also called a pharaoh.

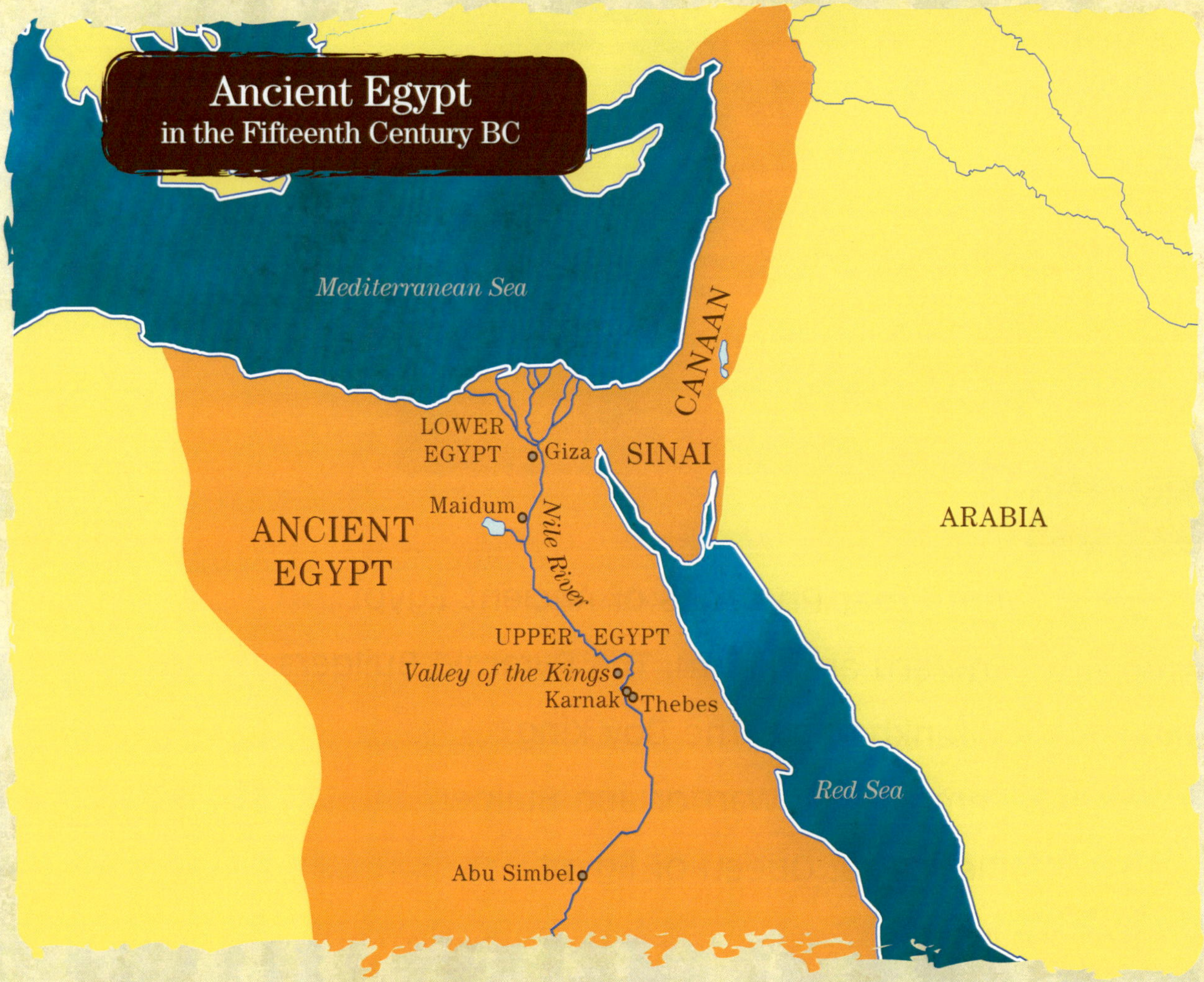

Ancient Egypt
in the Fifteenth Century BC

Mediterranean Sea
CANAAN
LOWER EGYPT
Giza
SINAI
Maidum
ANCIENT EGYPT
Nile River
ARABIA
UPPER EGYPT
Valley of the Kings
Karnak
Thebes
Red Sea
Abu Simbel

When a pharaoh died,
his **mummified** body was placed in a **tomb**.
Items such as jewellery, furniture and food
were also placed in the tomb,
to be used by the pharaoh
in his **afterlife**.

Cats were very important in Egyptian culture, and sometimes people had cats mummified and buried with them.

The ancient Egyptians believed that the gods brought them good luck, and the pharaoh was responsible for keeping the gods happy.

If the gods became angry, the people would blame the pharaoh and he would become less powerful.

a pharaoh making an offering to the god Osiris

Most years, the Nile River floods, providing water for nearby farmland.

If the Nile River did not flood,
the people thought that the gods were unhappy.
The people could not grow enough crops
to feed everyone if the Nile did not flood.

The pharaoh was also responsible
for protecting Egypt and its people from enemies,
and building up and sharing **resources**.

Most of Egypt's history centres around
the rule of each pharaoh's family,
or **dynasty**.

CHAPTER 2

Sneferu and Khufu: The Pyramid Builders

Sneferu was the first pharaoh
of the fourth dynasty
and he ruled from about 2613 BC to 2589 BC.
He helped build his empire
by trading with other countries.

He is famous for building many pyramids,
including the large pyramid at Maidum.

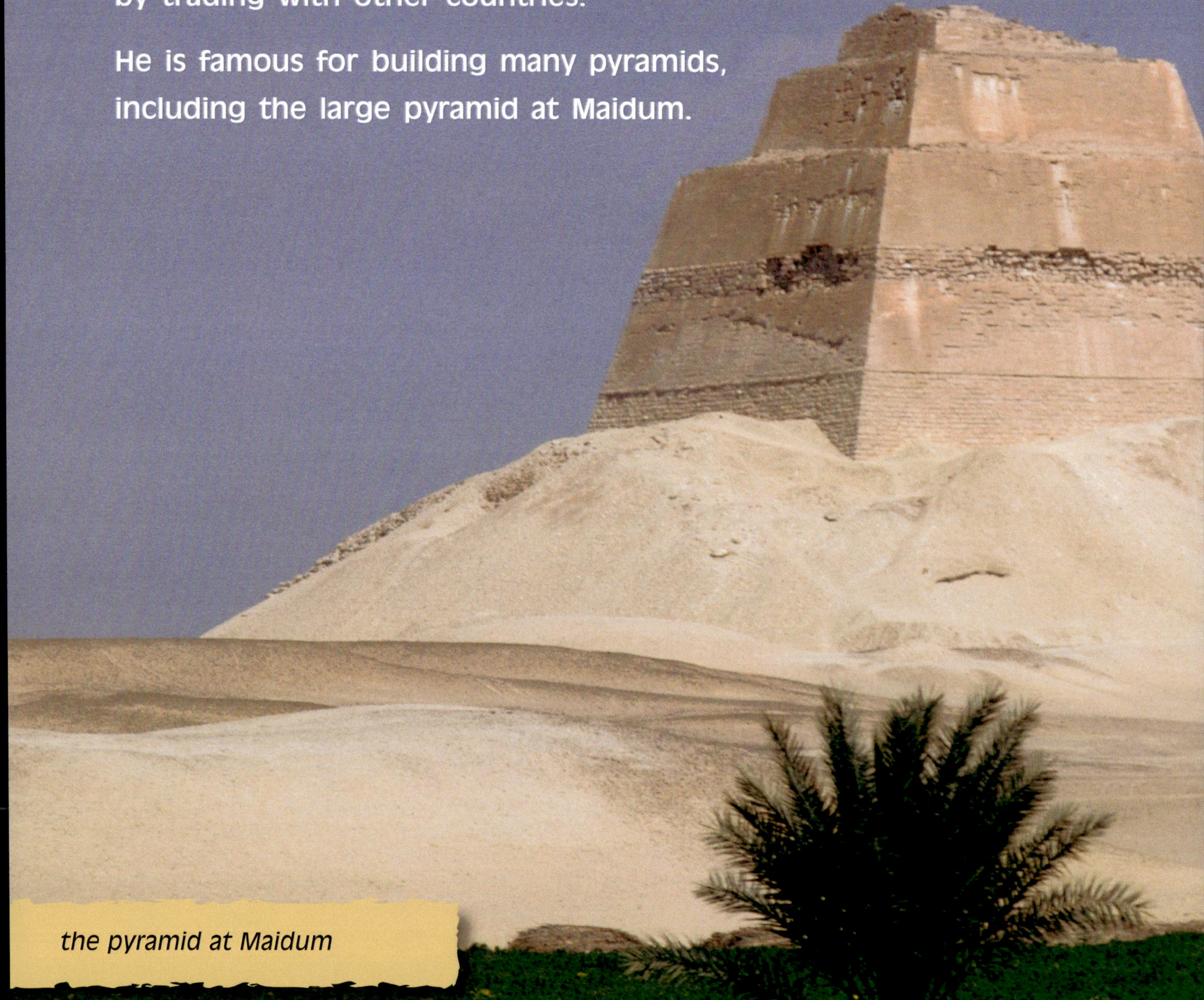

the pyramid at Maidum

Sneferu's son was Khufu,
who is sometimes called Cheops.
He is thought to have learned many
of his building skills
from his father.

a statue of Khufu

Khufu became known as one of Egypt's greatest pyramid builders.
He was in charge of building the Great Pyramid of Giza, which took about 20 years.
It is the largest pyramid in Egypt.

the Great Pyramid of Giza (middle)

The Great Pyramid was the tallest building in the world for 3800 years.

Khufu brought together thousands of workers
to help build the Great Pyramid.
It is thought that these people worked on the pyramid
when the Nile flooded each year
and no farming work could be done.

Two and a half million blocks of sandstone were used
to build the Great Pyramid.

CHAPTER 3

Tutankhamen: The Boy King

Tutankhamen ruled Egypt
during the eighteenth dynasty,
from about 1334 BC to 1325 BC.
He was only eight or nine years old
when he became pharaoh.
Tutankhamen ruled for only about nine
or ten years.

Like all pharaohs,
Tutankhamen was worshipped
by the ancient Egyptian people.
However, he was too young
to make important decisions
for the whole country,
so people from his government
made decisions for him.

Tutankhamen only became famous after his death, because of the large amount of treasure that was found in his tomb.

The tomb was discovered in the Valley of the Kings in 1922. It was believed to be in almost exactly the same state as it was over 3200 years ago.

Tutankhamen's mummy inside his tomb

the Valley of the Kings

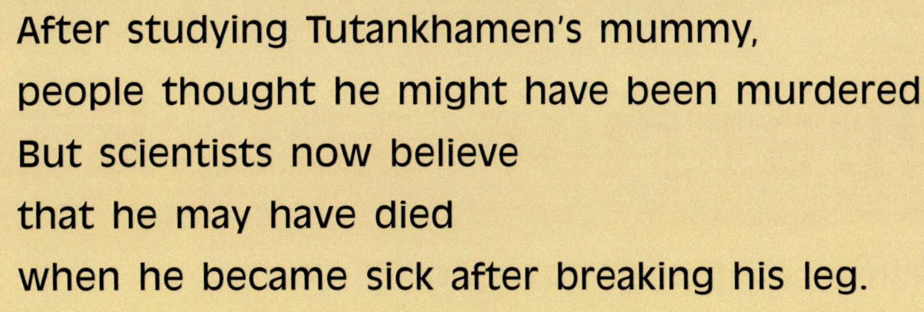

After studying Tutankhamen's mummy, people thought he might have been murdered. But scientists now believe that he may have died when he became sick after breaking his leg.

Tutankhamen's death mask

Ramesses II: Warrior and Builder

Ramesses II ruled Egypt for 66 years
from 1279 BC to 1213 BC,
during the nineteenth dynasty.
During his life,
Ramesses II had many wives
and 100 children.

Rameses II is remembered
as one of Egypt's most powerful rulers.
He was always trying
to make his empire bigger and stronger.
He was a good **warrior**
who won many battles,
and he enjoyed a life of great wealth.

Ramesses II built the temples
and buildings at Karnak.
But the buildings that he is best known for
are the temples cut into the sandstone rock face
at Abu Simbel.

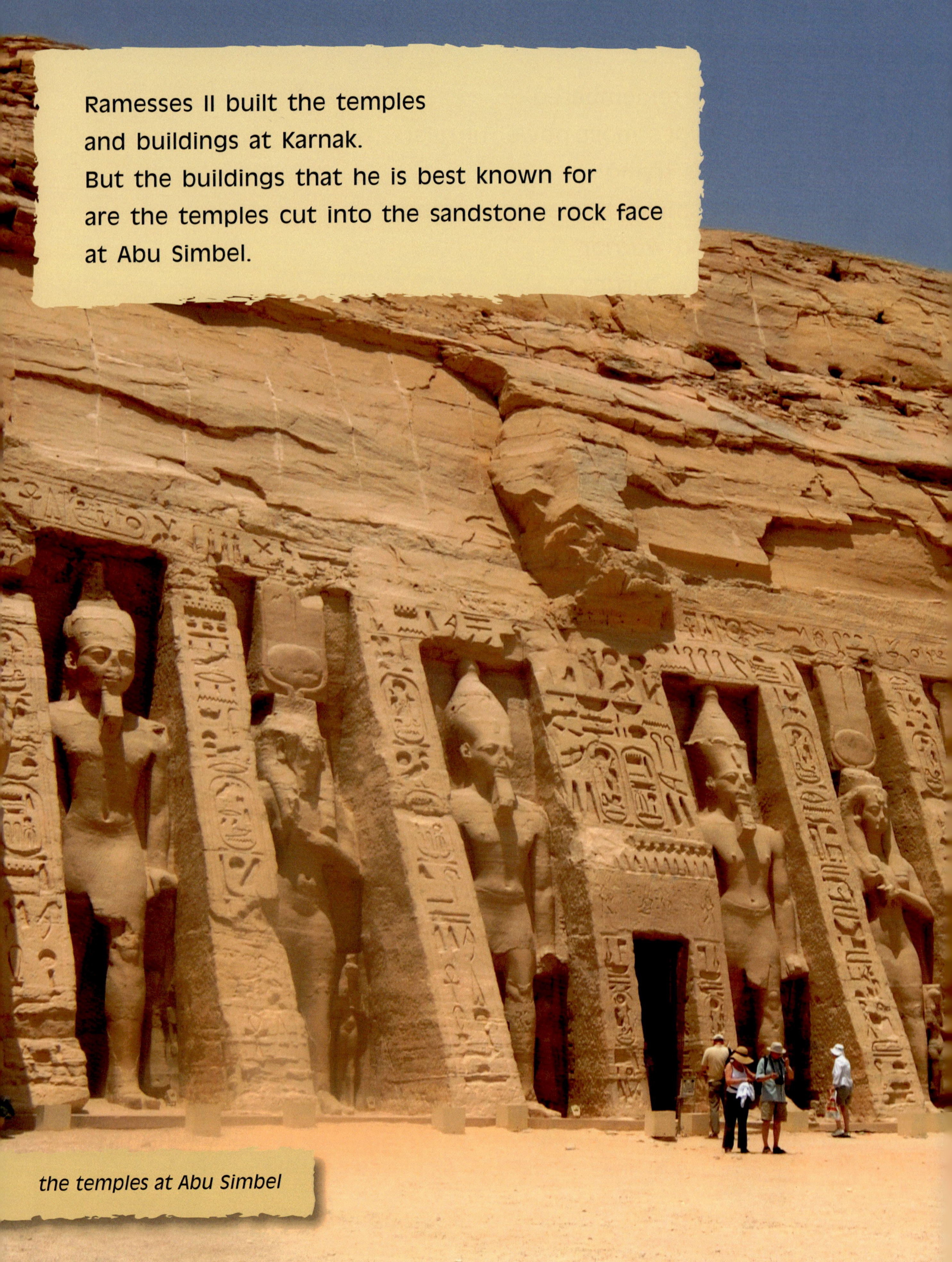

the temples at Abu Simbel

The tomb of Ramesses II was found in the Valley of the Kings, but it had been robbed and destroyed by floods.

the tomb of Ramesses II

However, his mummy was very well **preserved**. It can be seen in the Cairo Museum in Egypt.

Cleopatra: Queen of Egypt

Cleopatra is one of the most famous pharaohs of ancient Egypt.
She came to power in 51 BC at the age of 17.
She was the last pharaoh of the Ptolemaic dynasty.

Cleopatra had to share power with her brother Ptolemy XIII, because a woman was not allowed to rule Egypt alone.

Cleopatra

Ptolemy XIII

Ptolemy was only 12 years old,
so at first Cleopatra took charge of Egypt.

Many Egyptians were not happy about this,
and when Ptolemy turned 15,
Cleopatra was thrown out of Egypt.

At first, both Cleopatra's and Ptolemy's heads appeared on Egyptian coins. The relationship between the two pharaohs broke down after Cleopatra had coins made featuring only her head.

Cleopatra met and fell in love with two important Roman leaders. The first was the powerful Julius Caesar, who helped return her to power in Egypt by forcing Ptolemy to leave the country.

The second was Mark Antony, who went to war to try to take over the **Roman Empire** with Cleopatra's help.

When she became queen of Egypt again, Cleopatra worked hard to earn the respect of the people. But today she is best remembered for the love stories of her relationships with Julius Caesar and Mark Antony.

Julius Caesar

Mark Antony

Glossary

afterlife the life after death of a person's soul or spirit

ancient Egypt an ancient North African civilisation that had great knowledge of medicine, building and mathematics

dynasty a series of rulers from the same family

mummified made into a mummy, by drying and embalming

preserved kept from rotting; made to last a long time

resources the wealth of a country, including money and food

Roman Empire an empire covering a large part of Western Europe from 753 BC to 450 AD

tomb a structure, often dug out of rock or earth, built to contain a dead body

warrior a person who is experienced at fighting

Index